RISING ★ STARS

Hachette UK's policy is to use papers that are natural, renewable and recyclable products and made from wood grown in well-managed forests and other controlled sources. The logging and manufacturing processes are expected to conform to the environmental regulations of the country of origin.

ISBN: 9781398325548

Text © Steve Cole
Illustrations, design and layout © Hodder and Stoughton Ltd
First published in 2022 by Hodder & Stoughton Limited (for its Rising Stars imprint, part of the Hodder Education Group),
An Hachette UK Company
Carmelite House, 50 Victoria Embankment, London EC4Y 0DZ
www.risingstars-uk.com

Impression number 10 9 8 7 6 5 4 3 2 1
Year 2026 2025 2024 2023 2022

Author: Steve Cole
Series Editor: Tony Bradman
Commissioning Editor: Hamish Baxter
Illustrator: Miriam Serafin/Advocate Art
Educational Reviewer: Helen Marron
Design concept: Gary Kilpatrick
Page layouts: Rocket Design (East Anglia) Ltd
Editor: Amy Tyrer

With thanks to the schools that took part in the development of *Reading Planet* KS2, including: Ancaster CE Primary School, Ancaster; Downsway Primary School, Reading; Ferry Lane Primary School, London; Foxborough Primary School, Slough; Griffin Park Primary School, Blackburn; St Barnabas CE First & Middle School, Pershore; Tranmoor Primary School, Doncaster; and Wilton CE Primary School, Wilton.

A catalogue record for this title is available from the British Library.

Printed in the UK.

Orders: Please contact Hachette UK Distribution, Hely Hutchinson Centre, Milton Road, Didcot, Oxfordshire, OX11 7HH.

Telephone: (44) 01235 400555. Email: primary@hachette.co.uk.

MIX
Paper from
responsible sources
FSC™ C104740

Contents

1 The ghost of a coach

"I'm so glad it's the weekend!" said Rocco Pirelli, walking home from school. He couldn't wait to get home and read his latest comic book from the library, *Revenge From Space*.

"Same," said his sister, Ana. "My mates want me to play football down the park, but I've got loads of homework to do."

"Loads?" Rocco snorted. "You're only ten. You should try being eleven. That's when you *really* get loads of homework!"

Ana pretended to yawn really loudly – Rocco always made such a big deal about being in the year above her at school. "Actually, I don't mind this homework. It's history."

"How can it be history?" said Rocco with a wink. "You haven't done it yet!"

"Very funny," said Ana. She turned to him and pulled a face. But as she did so, she saw a strange patch of mist above the road.

"What's that, Rocco?" she said.

Rocco turned to see. He gasped. Something was pushing its way out of the glowing mist. Something sleek and shiny but strangely see-through. It had a large, curved windscreen and a row of six headlights.

"It looks like a coach coming from nowhere, hanging in mid-air?" Ana stared in amazement. "It's like the *ghost* of a coach!"

"It's coming towards us!" Rocco realised. "Run!"

The two of them sprinted away down the street. But the coach came soaring over their heads. Time seemed to slow down as a blaze of light surrounded the children. Rocco felt his feet leave the ground. Ana felt her long, dark hair standing on end.

Then the coach vanished ... taking Ana and Rocco with it!

"Dear, dear," came a high, tinny voice. *"This has never happened before!"*

Rocco opened his eyes. He was lying in an aisle between two rows of seats – like on a bus or an aeroplane. Someone was crouching over him.

It looked like a robot woman. She was wearing a smart, navy-blue uniform, like a flight attendant's. She had metal skin, long hair like tinsel and glowing eyes. On top of her head sat a small satellite dish.

"Please do not be afraid," the robot said. "You will be returned to your proper place and time as soon as possible."

"What!" spluttered Rocco. "Who are you? Where am I? How did I get here? What's happening? Where is Ana?"

"Question overload!" squeaked the robot. "I am Tori the tour guide. You are on board a Time Tours coach – for holidays in history. We were travelling from the future when our engines went wrong. We time-jumped into the 21st century by mistake and, er, accidentally sucked up you and your sister."

Rocco stared at her. "*What?*"

"I repeat, I am Tori the tour guide," said the robot. "You are on board a Time Tours coach—"

"I heard what you said," Rocco told her. "I just don't believe any of it."

"It's true." Tori gave a mechanical sniff. "I am a robot tour guide. I give facts – not fibs!"

"She told me the same story when I woke up a minute ago." Ana rose from a nearby seat, pushed past Tori and helped her brother up. "Oh, Rocco, I'm so glad you're here, too."

"*I'm* not!" twittered Tori. "Taking passengers from different time zones is against all the rules. We must return you quickly."

"Good," said Ana. "Our mum hates us being late home. She will be worrying."

"There's no need for anyone to worry – this is a time machine." Tori winked. "However long you spend here, we can drop you off in your own time, moments after you left!"

"Right. Sure you can. No problem," said Rocco, staring around. "Look at this place, Ana. It's like we've ended up in the pages of *Revenge From Space*. We've got to be dreaming!"

They sat down heavily. The inside of the coach looked like a spaceship. The driver was another robotic creature – he turned switches and levers instead of a steering wheel. The windscreen was filled with swirling patterns, like they were travelling through a tunnel of light. A gleaming gangway ran between two rows of purple plastic seats. The other passengers were all dressed in white plastic overalls with hoods. They watched Rocco and Ana nervously, as if afraid the children would bite.

"Everyone, stay in your seats," Tori told the passengers. "We will shortly be arriving in the year 1838. Then our driver will check the coach engines and make any repairs needed."

"1838?" Rocco laughed. "Seriously?"

"Queen Victoria's coronation!" said a boy in a nearby seat. "This time tour is 'The Royal Special'," he explained. "We started with King Grun marrying the Princess of Mars in 2743, and we'll end with William the Conqueror being crowned king in 1066."

"Wow!" Ana whistled. "That's awesome!"

"I'm Ifan," said the boy. "Do you really come from the 21st century? Do you live in a house with lots of rooms?"

"Not really *lots*," said Ana. "We have three bedrooms, a bathroom, a kitchen ..."

"SO MANY ROOMS!" Ifan marvelled. "I'm from the year 3000. The whole world is super-crowded – there are too many people and not enough space. We all live in tiny flats stacked up in towers that stand a mile high. There's nowhere to go, anywhere on Earth."

"Is that why you take holidays in history?" asked Rocco. "Because there's nowhere nice left to visit in your own time?"

"Exactly," said Ifan sadly. "My mum put me on this tour because it's educational. If I'm going back in time, I'd much rather just run around in a park. Or go to a beach. Or—"

BAM! The coach lurched suddenly and threw Rocco and Ana to the floor. The passengers screamed and shouted. An alarm went off.

"Attention!" said Tori. "The coach is running through time turbulence. Please do not be alarmed."

A moment later, the controls at the front exploded.

"All right, *NOW* you can be alarmed!" Tori shouted as the driver battled with the smoking controls. "Fasten your seat belts. This coach is out of control!"

2 Tomorrow is yesterday

Ana and Rocco clung on to each other as the coach spun around. The patterns of light on the windscreen sped past like burning clouds. The engines howled like invisible wolves. The passengers howled even more loudly.

Then there was a shrill chime. The engines grew quieter. The coach slowed its spinning.

"The driver has brought the coach under control!" cheered Tori.

CRASH! The coach shuddered to a stop.

"*Almost* under control," Tori added. She checked a chunky watch on her wrist. "The good news is that we have arrived in the right time and place! We are now close to Buckingham Palace in London at 9a.m. on Thursday 28th June 1838."

"What's the bad news?" called Ifan.

"The coach has broken down," Tori admitted.

Rocco frowned. "You mean we're stuck in the past?"

"I'm sure it won't be for long," said Tori, quickly. "I have sent an emergency call to Time Tours' head office. They will reply very soon."

The coach had landed beside a very wide road crowded with hundreds of people. Women wore smart dresses with puffy skirts. Men wore fancy suits. Horses and carts rattled past, and the sounds of cheers and chatter filled the air.

Ana was bursting with excitement. "We've really travelled back into the past!"

Tori's satellite dish was spinning round slowly. "Message from Time Tours," she announced. "A repair-bot has been sent from the year 3000. It will arrive ... now."

A second later, a bronze, human-sized robot in grey overalls appeared beside her and waved a spanner at them. "I need to check the nuclear fuel rods for damage," it said. "Everybody must leave the coach."

"Very well," said Tori. "Passengers! Before going out, please activate your wonder-onesies."

Rocco stared. "Your *what*?"

Ifan patted the white plastic suit he was wearing. He cleared his throat. "Wonder-onesie – dress me for London in June 1838!"

Suddenly, Ifan was wearing a short, blue jacket and dark trousers. His hair was neatly combed. The other passengers said the same words, and soon their outfits were changing, too.

"Wow!" Rocco's jaw dropped in amazement. "Brings a whole new meaning to wearing 'smart clothes'!"

"All part of the Time Tours service," said Tori, holding a wonder-onesie in each metal hand. "Here. Put these on."

Ana and Rocco quickly climbed into the plastic suits.

"Let's have a go," said Ana. "Wonder-onesie – dress me for London in June 1838!" The wonder-onesie glowed and, in a moment, she was wearing a pink dress. Her dark hair disappeared beneath a white bonnet. Even her trainers changed into chunky leather shoes. "This is like the wildest dressing-up box ever!" she said. "How do we change back again?"

"Just tell the wonder-onesie," said Ifan. "Your real clothes are stored in its memory as soon as you put it on."

"Wonder-onesie, dress me for London in 1838, too!" said Rocco. In a flash, he was wearing a black jacket with a grey shirt and grey trousers. "Ow, these clothes are all stiff and scratchy."

"That's the way clothes were in this time," Tori explained. She turned to the other passengers. "I'm about to open the doors. Queen Victoria will be leaving the palace shortly for her coronation. You can watch her go – but remember the Time Tours rules," she said sternly. "Stay close to the coach, and look but don't touch."

The coach doors hissed open, and the passengers trooped out.

"Come on," Ifan told Ana and Rocco. "Time to go Victorian!"

Ana and Rocco followed him outside. The pong of muck and unwashed bodies filled the air. Crowds of people lined the wide street and filled the parks beyond, cheering and waving Union Jack flags or bunches of flowers.

Everyone was looking at a grand, slightly soot-stained building at the end of the road: Buckingham Palace. Rocco recognised it from a sightseeing trip when he was younger – which was ... almost 200 years from now!

Ana looked back at the Time Tours coach. She gasped – it had gone! In its place was a long, wooden caravan with two horses.

"Don't worry, the coach is still there," said Ifan. "It *is* the caravan. It disguises itself wherever it lands so the locals don't get a shock."

Just then, the crowd roared with cheers and applause. Ana turned to find the royal carriage was being driven out of the palace with Queen Victoria inside!

The carriage was covered in gold leaf and shone in the sunlight. It was drawn by four fine, white horses, steered by coachmen dressed in red and gold. Ana beamed and waved along with everyone else. She glimpsed Queen Victoria inside – a short, dark-haired woman with big eyes – and was surprised at how young the ruler looked.

"Well," said Rocco. "I didn't expect to be saying 'Hi' to Queen Victoria when I left school this afternoon!"

"Imagine if we actually met her!" Ana laughed. "This is awesome. Do you think we can stay for the whole time tour?"

"I'm afraid not," came a squeaky voice behind them.

Rocco jumped to find Tori right behind them. She was wrapped up in a long cloak and hood so her silver skin didn't show.

"The repair-bot can't fix the coach here," Tori said. "It has to be time-towed back to the year 3000. We can stop in the 21st century on the way."

"Shame," said Rocco. "Zipping about through history sounds brilliant!"

"I wanted to enjoy all the space they had in earlier times," said Ifan sadly.

"There's not much of that here," said Ana.

"But there's a park just over there," Ifan said. "Let's go and hang out for a bit!"

"I guess this is our one chance to see a bit of Victorian London," said Ana.

"Okay," Rocco agreed. "But only a few minutes. We don't want to miss the coach!"

Ana, Ifan and Rocco moved quickly through the crowded street, past Buckingham Palace. Suddenly, a boy came running towards them, pushing and shoving through the crowds. He was dressed in dirty clothes with a grey scarf round his neck.

"Police! Clear the way!" came an angry shout. "Stop that boy!"

The boy pushed past Rocco and Ana, and then crashed into Ifan, knocking him into a dirty puddle. The boy stopped, panting for breath, and Ana stared at him in amazement.

3 Against the law!

"It's spooky," Ana told the boy. "You and Ifan could be twins."

"Ifan, is it?" smirked the boy. He tugged off his scarf and wrapped it around Ifan's neck. "Well, since we look so alike, I'll let the nice constable arrest you instead of me – so I can come back and rob the palace tonight!"

"Wait!" Ifan cried, scrambling up, wet and dirty. But the boy darted away into the crowd.

Rocco helped Ifan stand up, just as a very large police officer – with red cheeks and a huge moustache – appeared. He wore a blue coat and a tall top hat. "Aha!" The man grabbed Ifan's arms. "We've got you now, Tommy!"

"Get off!" Ifan tried to pull free. "My name's not Tommy!"

"This isn't the boy you were chasing," said Ana. "He ran off."

"Don't lie to me, nippers," the police officer said. "I'm Inspector Swann. I saw little Tommy Sweep here trying to break into Buckingham Palace while everyone's eyes were on the queen!"

"I told you," said Ifan. "I'm not Tommy Sweep."

"Thought I wouldn't recognise you in stolen clothes, did you? You forgot this." Swann tapped the dirty scarf around Ifan's neck. "Now, then. One of the palace servants told me that the key to the queen's jewellery chest was missing." He searched Ifan, then Rocco, then Ana. "Where is that key? Where did you hide it?"

"Tommy Sweep still has it," said Ana crossly. "He said he's coming back to rob the palace tonight."

Swann laughed. "There's no coming back from where *he's* going."

"But this isn't Tommy Sweep," said Rocco. "His name's Ifan. You have to believe us!"

"Why should I believe the likes of you?" said Swann, glaring at Rocco and Ana. "I know kids like you – you're happy to help any crook that throws you a coin. Just behave yourselves, or it'll be the lock-up for you – same as for Tommy here." Inspector Swann dragged Ifan away.

"Let me go!" Ifan squealed. "Help! I'm not supposed to go far from the coach ..."

"Now what do we do?" Ana said to Rocco. "The coach won't leave without us, will it?"

"Course not," said Rocco, wishing he felt as confident as he sounded. "Anyway, we can't leave Ifan in trouble like this."

"No way," Ana agreed. "Come on, let's follow."

Inspector Swann took Ifan to a blue police wagon parked in a side alley. It was full of children in scruffy clothes, guarded by more police officers in tall hats. The horses that pulled the wagon stamped their hooves on the cobbles, eager to set off. Swann pushed Ifan into the wagon. A thin police officer put handcuffs on him.

"Well done, sir!" The thin police officer gave Swann a salute. "Little Tommy Sweep, caught at last."

Rocco groaned. "We keep telling you, Tommy is still free. He's going to rob the palace tonight!"

"Nonsense, boy," said Swann. He smiled at the thin police officer. "Now take this bunch off to the *Dasher*!"

"The *Dasher*?" said Ifan. His eyes were wide with alarm. "What's the *Dasher*?"

But Inspector Swann had already turned and marched off down the street. The thin police officer pulled on the horses' reins.

Ifan stared helplessly at Rocco and Ana as he was taken off in the wagon.

"We'll get you out of this, Ifan!" Rocco yelled.

"There you are!" came a metallic squeal behind them. It was Tori, still wrapped up in her cape. "Wait. Where is Ifan?"

"Oh, Tori, he's been arrested!" Ana said. She and Rocco quickly told the robot what had happened.

"So, basically, the coach can't leave until we've rescued him," said Rocco.

"Er, about that …" Tori gave a mechanical sigh. "The coach has already been towed away."

Ana's eyes grew wider. "What about us?"

"I did tell you to wait beside the coach," Tori reminded them. "But don't worry. I stayed behind to look after you. Time Tours will send a time pod here as soon as they can – it's like a lifeboat for time travellers. Unfortunately, all the time pods are busy at the moment."

"So, Time Tours' coaches break down a lot?" said Ana gloomily.

"This is not untrue," Tori replied. "But we have a far better record than our competitors, Timely Trips!"

"And until this pod arrives, we are stuck in Victorian times," Ana added.

"Even worse, Ifan's been locked up in the *Dasher*," said Rocco. "Whatever that is."

"*Dasher* ... *Dasher* ..." Tori bleeped and blooped, and her satellite dish whirred. "Checking memory banks. Aha! *Dasher* was a ship first launched in 1797. When *Dasher* was no longer safe to sail at sea, she was used as a floating prison in the River Thames from 1832 onwards. She held criminals when the prisons were full."

"Wow, having a robot computer brain comes in handy," said Ana. "Which way is the *Dasher*?"

Tori pointed straight ahead.

"Finding Ifan is only the first part of the problem," said Rocco. "How are we ever going to bust him out of a Victorian prison?"

Ana gave her brother a smile. "Let's find out!"

4 Prison break!

Tori led Ana and Rocco to a row of large red-brick warehouses on the banks of the busy Thames. Small boats went back and forth in the afternoon light, collecting crates or dropping them off. Workmen used ropes to help lift bundles of spices or silk from the boats into the buildings.

The smell of the river made Ana feel sick. "Ugh! Why does it stink so much?" she asked, pinching her nose.

"Scanning memory banks," said Tori, bleeping. "London's sewers run straight into the river. Things will get even worse and smellier until 20 years or so from now when the sewers will be rebuilt."

"Remind me to come back then and take a holiday," said Rocco. "So, where's the *Dasher*?"

"There," said Tori, pointing downriver.

A huge ship loomed up from the water like an enormous wooden whale. It didn't have any sails. Ropes were strung between the short masts, draped with ragged prisoners' clothes that were drying in the smelly breeze. Guards in dark uniforms stood on the riverbank beside it.

"We'd better be careful," said Rocco. "They'll stick us in there *with* Ifan if we get caught trying to get him out."

Ana saw that on the opposite bank of the Thames there were only marshes. "Our only chance is to get to the far side of the *Dasher* so the guards can't see us," she said.

Rocco pointed to an old rowing boat, dumped and half-sunk in the water. "We can take this," he said, dragging it on to the riverbank. But there was a large hole in the rotting wood.

"That piece of junk won't take us anywhere!" said Ana.

"Or maybe it will," said Tori. She took a piece of shiny, smooth metal as big as her palm from under her cloak. "This is a patch I use for self-repairs. It should work on wood, too!" She pressed her hand to the metal, which began to melt. Soon the patch had mended the hole completely.

"Brilliant," breathed Ana.

Tori made a happy, burbling noise and held the boat while Ana and Rocco climbed in. Then she stretched out her silvery arms. "Here. You can use them as oars."

Rocco took hold of her left arm and pulled it off. "No 'arm in trying!" he said with a grin.

"Wait," said Ana, looking down at her ladylike clothes. "Dressed like this, we really stand out. Wonder-onesie – dress me like a prison guard from 1838!"

Her clothes blurred and in a moment she was dressed in a smart, black uniform with shiny brass buttons and a peaked cap.

"Good thinking," said Rocco. "Wonder-onesie – make me look like a prison guard in 1838!"

But it took much longer for his ragged outfit to change.

"Your wonder-onesie has a minor fault," Tori noted. "I hope it doesn't stop working."

"Me, too," said Rocco. "I don't really want it to turn back into a white plastic suit and shower cap – not a cool look!"

Ana took Tori's right arm and used it to push away from the riverbank.

It took a while to get used to rowing, but Ana and Rocco were soon working as one. Tori curled up in the boat beneath her cloak so no one could see her. Rocco kept an eye on the guards, but they seemed more interested in chatting than in keeping watch.

Close up to the *Dasher*, they could see that the timbers of the ship were rotten and crumbling. "No wonder this place isn't allowed on the sea any more," said Ana. "What a wreck!"

"Ifan?" Rocco called quietly. "Are you there?"

There was no answer. Ana steered the boat further along the side of the ship.

"Ifan," called Rocco again quietly. "Are you there?"

"Who's that?" came a whisper in reply. "Rocco? Is that you?"

"Yes!" Rocco looked up and saw Ifan's face peering out at them through a porthole in the side of the ship.

"We're here to rescue you," whispered Ana.

"Oh, thank you!" Ifan said gratefully. "It's horrible in here! It's crowded and dirty and it stinks. But I can't get out through that window."

Ana reached up and felt the wooden side of the ship. "Don't worry, Ifan," she said. "The timbers of this ship are super old and rotten. Tori, can you put your arms back on and help me and Rocco pull off some planks?"

"Then Ifan can climb out," Rocco agreed. "Good thinking!"

With her arms back in place, Tori used her strong metal fingers to prise off a rotten board just above the waterline.

"I'm nearly through!" Ifan hissed to them.

"Hey, what's going on in there?" came the shout of a guard, followed by a rattle of keys.

"Quickly!" hissed Ifan.

Rocco and Ana tore away half of another plank, and Ifan quickly wiggled through. Ana dragged him clear and into the boat.

"Hold on," said Tori. "Time for a fast getaway." She reached into the water at the back of the boat and paddled with her hands at super speed. The boat shot away like a torpedo.

A couple of minutes later, they reached the riverbank where they'd found their borrowed boat.

"Why did you let us row if you could do that, Tori?" asked Ana.

"Because now … my power is low," said Tori. Her voice sounded like it was playing at the wrong speed. "It will take time to recharge my batteries."

"Well, at least we've got Ifan back," said Rocco. "All we have to do is dodge the guards and stay out of sight until this time pod thing turns up and takes us all home."

"That is *not* all," said Tori. "I have checked my memory banks. Victorian newspapers said that Tommy Sweep was caught by Inspector Swann and arrested for robbery on 28th June 1838."

"Which is today," said Ana. "Tommy told us he was going back to the palace tonight."

"Makes sense," said Rocco. "On Coronation Day, everyone will be busy fussing over the queen and might not spot a burglary."

"Tommy's a horrible boy," said Ifan. "When he's caught, it will serve him right."

"But what if he *isn't* caught?" Tori gave an electronic sigh. "Inspector Swann thinks that *Ifan* is Tommy Sweep. He believes that Tommy is already locked up."

"But really, Tommy's still free," said Rocco. "And he still has that key to Queen Vic's jewellery chest."

Tori nodded weakly. "The robbery will still happen. Tommy won't be arrested. History will be changed."

"But does it matter if we've changed history a little bit?" Ana said.

"WHAT?" Tori shook with shock. "Of course it matters. Changing history is like throwing a pebble in a pond. The *PLOP* of the pebble may be small, but it still sends ripples through the water. Tommy not being arrested could lead to all sorts of changes that would alter the future as we know it."

"I see," said Ana. "You're saying the pond is history, and we're the pebble."

"I'm just glad I'm not the plop," said Rocco. "But I get it. Doing one little thing in the past can change the future in big ways."

"Exactly," said Tori. "That's why, as time travellers, we need to make sure that history stays on the right path. Somehow, we must make sure that Tommy Sweep is caught today, like history says he was."

Ana nodded. "We don't have long to set history back on the right track," she said. "Come on – back to Buckingham Palace!"

5 Break-in at Buckingham Palace

It was starting to get dark as the three children and Tori reached Buckingham Palace. Tori told them that a grand celebration dinner was being held in Queen Victoria's honour. Servants were buzzing between buildings like flies.

Rocco, Ana, Ifan and Tori peered through the railings that kept people out of the grounds.

"Maybe Tommy will be caught trying to get inside the palace," said Rocco hopefully. "Surely there's got to be top security?"

"Scanning memory banks," said Tori quietly; her batteries were recharging, but only slowly. "Security was *not* good in Queen Victoria's age. Newspapers say a boy called Thomas Jones broke into the palace *four* times!"

"I suppose children are small enough to get through the railings," Ana said.

"Look!" Ifan hissed, pointing into the gardens.

Ana and Rocco saw Tommy slink past a hedge and run towards the palace.

"We'll have to go in there after him," said Ana. "It's the only way to make sure Tommy is caught red-handed with the jewels."

"I can't go in," said Ifan. "Tommy and I look so much alike, I might get arrested again."

"And I must remain here," said Tori, tapping her satellite dish. "The time pod rescue ship will home in on me. It should arrive soon."

"Fingers crossed," said Rocco. He looked at Ana. "Looks like it's just you and me, sis."

"We'd better disguise ourselves," said Ana. "Wonder-onesie, dress me like a palace servant in 1838!" Her prison guard uniform glowed and shifted. Suddenly, she was wearing a black dress with a white pinny and a shawl around her head.

"Wonder-onesie, dress *me* like a palace servant, too," said Rocco. It took at least a couple of minutes for his guard uniform to transform into the red, gold and black royal uniform of a male servant.

"Your dodgy wonder-onesie is getting worse," said Ana.

"If it breaks down completely, press the top button to restart it," said Tori.

"How long will *that* take?" asked Rocco.

"No more than a few minutes. Perhaps ten." Tori paused, calculating. "Possibly fifteen."

"Great," Rocco sighed.

He and Ana took deep breaths and slipped through the railings. They crouched low as they followed Tommy Sweep's path through the gardens in the evening gloom. Rocco's heart was pounding. He was sure that police whistles would start blowing at any moment.

Round the back of the palace, Ana spotted a door left ajar. She and Rocco slipped inside.

"Wow," breathed Ana, staring around in wonder. The palace was beautiful, with lush carpets and chandeliers covered in dangling glass decorations. Oil lamps gave a smoky light, leaving soot and shadows on the walls.

They moved into the corridor. "Now where?" hissed Rocco.

Ana listened. In one direction, she heard music and noisy chatter. "The queen's party must be going on down there," she said. "I don't hear anything the other way."

"Let's get searching," Rocco said.

Ana and Rocco moved quietly through the dingy corridors. Sometimes they ran into palace staff carrying dishes, goblets and tablecloths. Luckily, no one challenged them – the celebration dinner was keeping everyone too busy, and they looked like servants hurrying along to help somewhere.

Suddenly, Rocco's uniform began to flicker. "Oh, no!" he groaned. "My wonder-onesie's losing power!"

The next moment he was back in the white plastic overalls.

"Great!" Rocco grumbled. "Now I totally stand out." He pressed a button near his collar. "Who knows how long it will take this rubbish wonder-onesie to restart!"

"Just stick to the shadows," Ana told him. "Come on."

Rocco and Ana reached the end of the corridor without finding anything. Then they heard the clunk of a key turning from behind a nearby door. It was quickly followed by a long, low creak.

Ana crept quietly up to the door and opened it just a crack. It led to an enormous, spotless bed chamber – Queen Victoria's room!

The carpet was pale yellow, patterned with beautiful red and blue flowers. There was a huge, fancy bed, as well as a settee and two armchairs. Beside the gigantic fireplace was a grand wooden chest.

And there was Tommy Sweep – gazing down at all the riches the queen kept inside the chest.

"Rocco, you stay here and keep an eye on him," whispered Ana. "I'm the one who looks like a servant, so I'll go and tell someone there's a thief in the queen's bedroom."

"I guess it would be hard for me to explain why I'm dressed as a shower curtain," said Rocco. "Okay, I'll watch Tommy. Get going!"

Ana rushed away down the corridor. Rocco kept on spying at the door.

Tommy started stuffing jewels down his shirt front. "I'd love to see the look on old Inspector Swann's face when he finds out what I've done," he muttered. "And when I've got all the queen's loot, I'll get out by climbing up her chimney!"

Just then, Rocco's wonder-onesie gave a quiet *BONG!*

Tommy heard and cocked his head. "What was that?"

Stupid onesie, thought Rocco. *It's given me away!*

Tommy started walking towards the door ...

6 Getaway!

Taking a deep breath, Rocco threw open the door before Tommy reached it. "Surprise!" he cried.

"You!" Tommy stared. "You were in the street this morning, with that boy who looked like me."

"The boy *you* got arrested to save your own skin," said Rocco, walking inside. "You'd have left him to rot on the *Dasher* for ever."

"Well, unless you can climb chimneys the way I can, *you're* the one who's going to get caught and blamed for this." Tommy smirked. "Maybe they'll lock you up on the same old wreck as your mate. Don't worry, it's bound to sink soon ... and glub, glub, glub – down you'll go!"

"You're the one who's going down," Rocco warned him.

Tommy stomped towards him. Rocco grabbed a stool and threw it in the boy's path. Tommy tripped over it, and gemstones scattered across the carpet as he fell. Rocco quickly grabbed a blanket from the queen's bed and threw it over Tommy's head.

With a roar of anger, Tommy wriggled out and picked up a heavy vase.

If he gets me with that and escapes up the chimney, I really am sunk! thought Rocco. Then he remembered the way his wonder-onesie had chimed.

It must have restarted!

"Speaking of 'sunk'," Rocco said. "Wonder-onesie, dress me as a Victorian deep-sea diver!"

In a flash of light, he was wearing a heavy diving suit with a big, round, brass helmet – exactly as he'd imagined. Tommy threw the vase, but it hit the helmet and broke into pieces.

Tommy yelled in terror as the door burst open to reveal Inspector Swann – with Ana right beside him!

"Bless my soul," said the inspector, his cheeks red and moustache quivering. "You were right, girl! I came here for dinner at the palace – I didn't expect to find a villain in the queen's bedroom! As well as, um … a diver?"

"It came out of nowhere!" cried Tommy. "Help!"

"You seem to have been helping yourself!" said Swann, pointing to the jewels spilling from Tommy's shirt. "You're under arrest for breaking into Buckingham Palace and trying to rob the queen!"

"Nice one, Inspector!" Rocco pulled off the heavy diving helmet and waved at Swann. "Good to see you again!"

Swann blinked. "You're the children from earlier? Extraordinary!"

Ana smiled. "We told you that the boy you caught wasn't Tommy Sweep."

"You did, girl, and I'm sorry," said Swann. "I will set your friend free as soon as I can."

"Um, yes," said Rocco. "You do that." He wasn't about to tell Swann that Ifan had already escaped that afternoon!

Swann frowned. "I don't understand what's gone on today ... but the important thing is that you've helped me catch this rotter." He removed the jewels from Tommy's shirt front, and then four royal footmen came into the room. The inspector turned to them. "Kindly deliver Tommy Sweep to my friends at the police station," he said. "They'll take good care of him."

The footmen nodded and dragged Tommy away.

"That's Tommy taken care of!" Ana grinned. "But tell me, Rocco, why are you dressed as a diver?"

Rocco laughed. "Because when I saw Tommy, I got a sinking feeling!"

Ana groaned. That had to be her brother's worst joke of the day.

Then everyone fell silent as a small, dark-haired woman swept into the room in a magnificent white dress.

"Your Majesty!" Swann bowed low. "Forgive us for entering your bedroom."

"You're Queen Victoria!" Ana gasped and grinned, and quickly did a curtsey. "This is amazing."

Rocco bowed, as best he could in his diving suit. "Pleased to meet you, Your Majesty!"

"What has happened here?" Queen Victoria demanded. "Why are my gems all over the floor?"

Swann smiled. "Ma'am, these children have risked their safety to protect your jewels from a wicked thief."

"Is that so?" Queen Victoria smiled at Rocco and Ana. "Well, then ... on this special day, I think it is only right I reward you – with a royal handshake."

She offered her hand to Ana and then Rocco. Each of them shook it with a smile.

"I wish I had a phone to take a selfie," said Rocco.

"A *what?*" Queen Victoria frowned. But before she could say any more, a rushing wind whipped through the room and a strange machine appeared beside the bed. It looked like a gold submarine and was as big as a car.

Queen Victoria and Inspector Swann gasped in surprise. But Rocco and Ana whooped for joy to see the words 'TIME TOURS' on the side of the craft.

"It's the time pod!" said Ana.

A door in the time pod slid open – to reveal Tori and Ifan.

"Cooeeee," called Tori.

"Your lifeboat's here," said Ifan. "Get in, quick!"

Rocco and Ana tumbled into the pod. The door slid shut behind them, and the rescue pod disappeared.

Queen Victoria and Inspector Swann were left staring at thin air.

"I think it is best that we say nothing of what happened here," said Queen Victoria.

"Yes, Your Majesty," said Inspector Swann. "Whatever you say!"

Rocco hugged Tori. "Nice timing," he said. "Glad to see you're feeling better."

"I plugged myself into the time pod for super-fast charging," she told them.

"Was that Queen Victoria I just saw?" asked Ifan.

Rocco and Ana explained what had happened.

"Well done," said Tori. "You've definitely put history back on track."

"So, what's the next stop?" asked Rocco.

"The 21st century for you and the year 3000 for me, I suppose," said Ifan. "And I won't moan about having no space at home now – not after sharing a cell with 25 other kids on the *Dasher*!"

"Tori," asked Ana, "can you really drop off Rocco and me to just a minute after we left?"

"Of course," said Tori.

"Then ... could we take the *long* way back to the future and see a bit more of the past first?" Ana went on.

Rocco grinned. "It would be the best history lesson I've ever had!"

"Well, I *am* a tour guide ... and there's no harm in a bit of adventure." Tori's satellite dish spun about while she thought. "Very well," she said with her brightest smile. "We will delay our return home for a little while longer and continue our time tour."

"Yay!" Ana cheered. "Watch out, history. Here we come again!"

Chat about the book

1 Read Chapter 3. What was the Dasher?

2 Go to page 39. Which word tells you that Tommy moved quietly and carefully in the palace grounds?

3 Read pages 10 and 11. Why did Ifan say he would prefer to run around in a park or go to the beach?

4 Go to the end of Chapter 1. How does the author want you to feel?

5 Read pages 20 and 21. What do we learn about Tommy?

6 Many Victorian children had to work. What do you think Tommy did? How do you know?

7 What is a 'wonder-onesie'? How did Rocco and Ana feel about their 'wonder-onesies'?

8 Would you like to go back in time and visit Victorian London? What would you like or dislike?